TESSA KRAILING

The Petsitters Club

8. Where's Iggy?

Illustrated by Jan Lewis

BARRON'S

First edition for the United States, Canada, and the Philippine Republic published by Barron's Educational Series, Inc., 1999

First published in Great Britain in 1998 by Scholastic Children's Books, Commonwealth House, 1-19 New Oxford Street, London WC1A 1NU, UK
A division of Scholastic Ltd

All inquiries should be addressed to:

Barron's Educational Series, Inc.
250 Wireless Boulevard
Hauppauge, New York 11788
http://www.barronseduc.com
ISBN 0-7641-0693-7
Library of Congress Catalog Card No. 98-45197

Library of Congress Cataloging-in-Publication Data
Krailing, Tessa, 1935–
    The Petsitters Club. 8. Where's Iggy? / Tessa Krailing ; illustrated by Jan Lewis.
        p. cm.
    Summary: Jovan is dismayed when the Petsitters Club is asked to look after a hamster and an iguana at the same time, as he dislikes both animals.
    ISBN 0-7641-0693-7
    [1. Clubs—Fiction. 2. Hamsters—Fiction. 3. Iguanas—Fiction. 4. Pets—Fiction.] I. Lewis, Jan, ill. II. Title. III. Title: Petsitters Club, 8. IV. Title: Where's Iggy?
PZ7.K85855Wh   1999
[Fic]—dc21   98-45197
                                                                          CIP
                                                                          AC

Printed in the United States of America
9 8 7 6 5 4 3 2

Chapter 1

Hamster Mystery

Jovan was NOT having a lucky day!

At lunchtime his father—Mr. Roy, the vet—brought home a small cage and put it on the kitchen table.

"Somebody left this in my veterinary office this morning," he said. "Just dumped it in a corner of the waiting room and vanished."

Jovan peered into the cage. All he could see was a pile of hay bedding, a water bowl and an exercise wheel. "What is it?" he asked.

"A hamster. I thought the Petsitters might like to look after him while we try to find the owner."

Jovan wrinkled his nose. He didn't know about the other three Petsitters, but personally, he didn't like hamsters. They had very sharp front teeth.

"Why was he left at your office?" he asked. "Is there something wrong with him?"

Dad shook his head. "I've checked him over and he seems healthy enough."

"Perhaps he bites or something," Jovan suggested.

"On the contrary, he's a friendly little fellow. And he's obviously used to being handled." Dad opened the cage and moved aside the bedding.

A small nose appeared, nervously twitching. Jovan put a cautious hand into the cage and stroked the top of the hamster's head.

"Don't you have any idea who left him there?" he asked.

"No, it's a mystery. If his owner doesn't come back, I'll try to find another home for him. Meanwhile it's over to the Petsitters." Dad closed the cage and handed it to Jovan.

Jovan sighed. "I'll take it over to Sam's house," he said. "Matthew wants us all to meet him there at three-thirty. He says he's got some important news."

He was the first to arrive at Sam's house.

"What have you got there, Jo?" Sam asked when she saw the cage.

"A hamster," said Jovan. "Someone dumped it at my dad's veterinary office. He wants us to look after it while he tries to find the owner."

"Poor little thing." Sam peered into the cage. "I love hamsters."

"I don't," said Jovan. "Can I leave him with you, please?"

"If you like. Have you got some food for him?"

Jovan held up a packet of hamster mix. "Dad gave me this."

"Oh, good. And we have plenty of fresh vegetables in the garden, so that should be all we need."

Matthew arrived next with his young sister Katie.

"Matthew's being really mean," Katie complained. "He keeps saying he's got important news, but he won't tell me what it is."

"I wanted to wait till we're all together." Matthew looked rather red in the face, as if he was about to burst. "You'd better sit down. I warn you, this will knock your socks off."

They all sat down around the kitchen table, staring at Matthew. "Go on, then," said Sam. "Knock our socks off."

Matthew drew a deep breath. But before he could speak, Katie spotted the cage Jovan was holding.

"What have you got there, Jo?" she asked.

"A hamster," said Jovan. "Someone dumped it at my dad's office, but he doesn't know who."

Katie peered into the cage. "What's his name?"

"He hasn't got one."

"Don't be silly, he must have a name," said Katie. "You'll have to give him one."

Jovan said doubtfully, "I suppose we could call him Hammy."

Katie wrinkled her nose. "Too ordinary. Why don't you call him George? Or William? Or —"

"Do you *mind?*" Matthew said impatiently. "I'm trying to tell you something important. We've been asked to look after a pet that's a lot more interesting than a hamster. A lot, lot, lot, lot, *lot* more interesting."

"Okay, so what is it?" asked Sam.

Quickly, before anyone else could interrupt, Matthew said, "An iguana."

The others stared at him. "A *what?*" asked Jovan.

"An iguana," Matthew repeated. "It belongs to a friend of our dad's. He's a policeman, like our dad, and he's got to go away to police school for five days. Yesterday evening he came over to our house—"

"I know who you mean!" said Katie. "Bill Wilkins. I saw him when I was playing in the garden."

Matthew went on. "He came to ask our dad if the Petsitters could keep an eye on his iguana while he's away. Dad said yes, he didn't see why not. So we've got the job!"

Jovan's heart sank. He had seen iguanas on television, big scaly reptiles with jagged teeth like crocodiles. One lash of their tails could take a man's arm off.

"Sorry, can't help," he said quickly. "I'll be too busy looking after this hamster."

Sam looked at him in surprise. "I thought you were going to leave him with me."

"I've changed my mind," he said.

The truth was, he'd much rather look after one small, timid hamster than a huge, jaw-snapping iguana!

"I wish you'd all stop rambling on about hamsters," said Matthew. "Bill Wilkins goes away tomorrow, and Dad promised him we'd stop by this afternoon for a briefing."

"What's a briefing?" asked Sam.

"Police talk," Matthew explained. "It means he's going to tell us what he wants us to do." He got up from the table. "Coming?"

Jovan was about to say no when he caught the stern look in Matthew's eye. Reluctantly he picked up the hamster's cage and followed the others out of the house.

No doubt about it, this was NOT his lucky day.

Chapter 2

Iguana Briefing

From the outside, Officer Wilkins's house looked quite ordinary, not at all the sort of house where you'd expect to find an iguana. Matthew opened the gate and walked up the path, followed by the other three Petsitters.

"Better keep that hamster out of sight, Jo," he warned as he rang the doorbell.

"It might get eaten."

Jovan looked horrified. He thrust the cage behind his back.

Matthew grinned. "Only joking! Iguanas are vegetarians."

Officer Wilkins opened the front door. "Hello, Matthew," he said. "Come inside."

They stepped into the hall. It was narrow and rather dark.

"These are the other Petsitters," said Matthew. "This is Sam and that's Jovan — his dad's Mr. Roy, the vet — and you already know my sister Katie. We've come for a briefing."

"Come into the greenhouse," said Officer Wilkins. "That's where I keep Iggy in the summer months."

They followed him through the living room to the greenhouse.

After the darkness of the house, the sunlight streaming through glass dazzled their eyes. The only shade came from huge potted plants.

"It's like the jungle!" Katie exclaimed.

"Iggy has to be kept warm," said Officer Wilkins. "That's why he lives in this heated terrarium."

He pointed to a large tank with sliding doors and a heat lamp fitted to the lid.

Inside the tank was a bare tree branch, a shallow tray filled with water — and an iguana.

Matthew bent down for a closer look. "He's got very long claws. I suppose he uses them for climbing."

"He's a beautiful color," said Katie. "I didn't expect him to be so green."

"He looks sort of prehistoric," said Sam. "Like a dinosaur."

Jovan didn't say anything. He stayed at the back of the room, clutching the hamster cage nervously to his chest.

"How big is he?" asked Sam.

"About twenty inches, counting his tail." Officer Wilkins sounded very proud of his pet. "He's still quite young. I haven't had him long. In fact this'll be the first time I've ever gone away and left him."

"We'll look after him for you," said Matthew confidently. "What do you want us to do?"

"Just come in every day and feed him," said Officer Wilkins. "He doesn't eat a lot, mainly cabbage leaves and bananas. He loves bananas. Oh, and crickets."

"Crickets?" Katie stared at him. "You don't mean *live* ones?"

"Yes, I keep them in this box." He picked up a cardboard box and opened the lid.

Katie peered inside. "I thought iguanas

were supposed to be vegetarians," she said in a small, quavery voice.

"Mainly they are," said Officer Wilkins. "But Iggy likes an occasional meaty snack."

"What about fresh water?" Matthew asked hurriedly, fearing that Katie was about to burst into tears. She loved all creepy-crawlies and couldn't bear for them to be killed.

"The tray needs changing every day," said Officer Wilkins. "He tends to bathe in it as well as drink it, so it can get pretty mucky. But you don't need to worry about the heating. The lamp switches on and off automatically."

Matthew gazed into the tank. The iguana gazed back at him unblinkingly with small lidded eyes. Sam was right, Iggy did look like a prehistoric monster.

Suddenly it occurred to him that all this feeding and watering business would mean putting his hand into the terrarium . . . .

"Is he friendly?" he asked Officer Wilkins.

"Oh, yes. He loves people. I'll take him out so you can have a closer look." Officer Wilkins opened the sliding door and reached inside. He picked up the iguana carefully and held him like a baby.

The Petsitters — except for Jovan — crowded around. "Can we pet him?" asked Sam.

"Yes, but don't make any sudden moves," warned Officer Wilkins. "Matthew, would you please close the door to the living room? If he gets away in here it doesn't matter, but if he runs into the house, it could take days to catch him. Once he even tried to climb up the chimney, but luckily I managed to coax him down."

"Can he run fast?" asked Sam.

"Very!" Officer Wilkins set the iguana down on the floor. For a moment Iggy remained still as a statue. Then, with surprising speed, he darted across the floor and started climbing the trunk of a large umbrella plant.

"You see?" Laughing, Officer Wilkins caught him and put him back in the terrarium. "Come into the kitchen. I'll show you where I keep his food."

At last the briefing was over. Officer Wilkins gave Matthew a door key and a telephone number where he could be contacted in case of trouble. "Not that I expect you'll have any," he said. "Just be sure to keep the terrarium door closed at all times, especially when you change his water."

"We'll be careful," Matthew promised.

As they walked down the path, Katie muttered, "I don't mind feeding him bananas, but I *won't* feed him live crickets! That's murder."

Chapter 3

"I'm Being Followed!"

On the way home, Jovan stopped at Sam's house to get the hamster food and some fresh spinach.

"Are you *sure* you want to look after him?" Sam asked.

"Quite sure," he said firmly.

Compared with an iguana, he thought, looking after a hamster would be a piece of cake.

He left Sam's house, carefully carrying the cage. "Well, if Officer Wilkins can call his iguana Iggy, I don't see why you can't be Hammy," he told the hamster. "Don't be scared, Hammy. You'll be safe with me until we find your owner."

He turned left at the end of Sam's road into Morton Avenue. It was a quiet road with hardly any traffic. Suddenly he thought he heard footsteps behind him.

He swung around quickly, but there was no one in sight, except a dog sniffing around a streetlight. That's funny, he thought, and hurried on.

After a moment he heard the footsteps again and swung around.

Nobody there.

Only the dog, sniffing at a fence.

He turned left into Beech Road, where he lived. By now he was hurrying as fast as he could without jiggling Hammy's cage too much. The footsteps hurried, too. When he reached his own front gate, he stopped and turned around quickly, hoping to take whoever it was by surprise.

Nobody there.

Only the dog, sniffing at the trunk of a tree.

Jovan was mystified. Surely the footsteps couldn't belong to the dog. It was a medium-sized dog, brown and white, with long ears and a pointed nose. But why was it following him? Could it be a *bloodhound*?

He raced up the front path, around the back and into the house, slamming the door behind him.

"Jo?" called his mother. "Is that you?"

He put Hammy's cage down on the kitchen table and went into the living room. His mother sat on the sofa, reading the newspaper, but he didn't speak to her. Cautiously he approached the window and peered out.

Nobody there.

Only the dog, sniffing at the front gate.

It had tracked him right to his own home! Hastily Jovan dodged back out of sight.

"*What* is the matter?" asked Mom.

"I'm being followed," he told her.

She put down the newspaper, looking alarmed. "Followed? Who by?"

"A dog. He's out there now, on the front path." He gulped. "I — I think it's a bloodhound."

Mom stood up and peered out. "That's not a bloodhound. It's a cocker spaniel." She opened the window. "Shoo! Go away!"

Jovan looked over her shoulder. "Are you *sure* it's only a cocker spaniel?"

"Quite sure. Anyway, it's run off now."
She closed the window.

"Phew!" Now that the danger was over
his knees felt quite shaky. "Why do you
think it followed me?"

"Maybe it was lost." She looked
concerned. "Poor thing, I shouldn't have
shooed it away. We should have taken it
to the police station. Jo, you'd better go
and see if it's still around."

Reluctantly he went to the front door
and looked out.

Nobody there.

Only a girl with red hair running around the corner.

He breathed a sigh of relief and closed the door. "It's gone," he told his mother.

"Oh, dear. I hope it's all right." She still looked concerned, so he told her about the iguana, hoping to take her mind off the dog. And when he'd finished telling her about the iguana, he took her to see the hamster.

By now it was early evening and Hammy had woken up. Jovan opened the door and took him out. Such a tiny little body, with small pink claws and a pink woffly nose. He clung tightly to Jovan's sweater, twitching his whiskers.

"I bet he's hungry," said Jovan. "How much of this hamster food do you think I should give him?"

"I'm not sure," said Mom. "Better wait till your father comes home. He'll tell you exactly how much."

Mr. Roy seemed pleased that Jovan had decided to look after the hamster after all. He told him to wash the spinach well and put a small handful of hamster mix into the bowl. "If he eats it all up you can give him some more. But watch that he isn't storing it in his cheek pouches."

"Did you find out who owned him?" asked Jovan.

"Not yet," said Mr. Roy. "If nobody claims him within a week I'll put up a sign in the waiting room. We'll soon find him a good home, don't worry."

Jovan gazed into the cage. Hammy was using his exercise wheel, his tiny feet scampering like crazy. He looked perfectly happy and contented. Perhaps, if they never found his owner . . .

"A funny thing happened today," said Mom. "Jovan was followed home by a stray dog. Have you heard if anyone's lost a brown-and-white cocker spaniel?"

Mr. Roy looked thoughtful. "Mrs. Tripp at the bookstore has a brown-and-white cocker spaniel. But I saw her today, and she didn't mention it was lost."

"It's a bit of a mystery," said Mom. "Jo, tell your father about the iguana."

Jovan was only too glad to tell his father about the iguana. Anything rather than talk about that snoopy dog who had followed him home.

But when he got to bed that night, he couldn't stop thinking about it. What if his mother was wrong about it being a cocker spaniel? It had behaved far more like a bloodhound, sniffing away as if it was following a scent. <u>His</u> scent! What's more, it had tracked him right home, so now it knew where he lived.

And who did those footsteps belong to — the Invisible Man?

Chapter 4

A Big Responsibility

"It's a big responsibility for you Petsitters," Matthew's dad said next morning at breakfast. "Having Officer Wilkins's key and going in every day to check on his iguana. I hope you won't let me down."

Matthew shook his head. "Don't worry, Dad. We'll be careful."

He began to feel quite nervous. This afternoon the Petsitters would have to visit Officer Wilkins's house . . . and go into the greenhouse . . . and open the door of the terrarium . . . and change Iggy's water without letting him out. Because if they *did* let him out, he might escape and climb up the chimney. Dad was right: it was a HUGE responsibility.

"It eats crickets," muttered Katie.

Dad looked puzzled. "What does?"

"The iguana." She sounded tearful. "I think it's cruel."

"Yes, well . . . Nature can be very cruel at times." Dad got up from his chair. "I must get to work. See you this evening."

As the day went on, Matthew felt more and more nervous. At three-thirty he went into the hall and called, "Katie! It's time we went over to Officer Wilkins's house to feed Iggy."

Katie's head appeared around the kitchen door. "I'm not coming."

"You must! We've all got to go. You heard what Dad said — this job is a big responsibility."

"I don't care," said Katie obstinately. "I'm not going to watch poor little crickets being gobbled up alive. I'd be sick!"

"We don't need to feed him any crickets," Matthew argued. "Officer Wilkins said they were only an occasional snack. We'll just give him cabbage leaves."

"I'm still not looking after any creature that's cruel enough to eat poor defenseless insects. You'll have to go without me." She slammed the door.

Matthew sighed. Never mind. Three Petsitters should be enough to feed Iggy without any problems. He set off for Jovan's house.

Jovan came to the front door. He peered past Matthew into the street, as if he expected to see someone else. "Sorry," he muttered. "Can't come."

"Why not?" demanded Matthew.

"I'm too busy looking after Hammy. Er, did you happen to notice a bloodhound hanging around outside?"

"No, I didn't!" Matthew began to feel annoyed. "An iguana isn't just any old pet, you know. It's a big responsibility. I can't feed him on my own."

"Sam will help you. Bye, Matthew." Jovan shut the door.

By now Matthew was in a bad mood. He stomped down the path and clanged the front gate behind him. "Stupid idiots!" he muttered.

Suddenly he realized someone was staring at him — a red-haired girl with a brown-and-white cocker spaniel. She must have been hiding behind the fence and overheard what he said.

"Hello, did you want something?" he demanded.

"N – n – no. . . ." She looked scared.

"Then scram," he said rudely.

Without another word she turned and fled down the road, followed by the dog.

Matthew felt ashamed of himself. He shouldn't have been so rude. To make things worse, he was sure he'd seen her before somewhere. . . .

Still feeling ashamed, he continued on his way to Sam's house.

He rang the bell twice but nobody answered. After the third time Sam's father came to the door looking dazed.

Matthew guessed he must be working on the cartoon strip he wrote for a magazine.

"Sorry to bother you," he said. "I've come to get Sam."

"She's not here." Sam's father scratched the top of his head. "I'm not sure where she went. Down to the shops, I think."

Matthew's heart sank. "Do you know how long she'll be?"

"No idea. Can I give her a message?"

"Yes, please. Tell her I've gone over to Officer Wilkins's house to feed his iguana."

"Iguana?" Sam's father looked more interested. "You're petsitting an iguana?"

Matthew nodded. "It's a big responsibility. I don't really want to do it on my own but — well, none of the others wants to come. So when Sam gets back will you tell her to hurry, please?"

Sam's father said he would and closed the door.

Matthew drew in a deep breath. It seemed he had no choice. He would have to visit Officer Wilkins's house by himself. And go into the greenhouse . . . and open the door of the terrarium . . . and change Iggy's water without letting him escape up the chimney.

This was a big responsibility he really DID NOT WANT!

Chapter 5

Iguana on the Run

Matthew opened the door of the greenhouse and looked inside. Katie was right when she said it was like the jungle, green and shady and mysterious. He felt like an explorer as he ventured inside. An explorer hunting for a wild beast. He bent down and peered into the terrarium.

Iggy was sitting still as a statue on the bare tree branch. He didn't look exactly pleased to see Matthew, but then, it was hard to tell with iguanas.

Slowly Matthew slid back the door of the tank.

Iggy didn't move.

Very, very slowly he reached inside for the water tray.

Still Iggy didn't move.

Matthew grabbed the water bowl and shut the door.

Phew! So far, so good.

He went into the kitchen and filled the tray with fresh water. He collected some cabbage leaves and went back to the greenhouse, taking care to close the door into the living room.

Slowly he opened the sliding door.

Iggy didn't move.

Very, very slowly he put the tray inside with the cabbage leaves.

Still Iggy didn't move.

He closed the door. Phew!

Then he remembered Officer Wilkins saying how much Iggy liked bananas. *"He has a banana every day,"* he'd said. Maybe that was why Iggy was still looking at him, not moving an inch. He was waiting for his banana.

Matthew went back to the kitchen and got a banana. He returned to the greenhouse, again taking care to close the door into the living room.

Slowly he opened the sliding door of the tank.

Iggy didn't move.

Very, very slowly he put the banana inside.

Still Iggy didn't move.

Maybe he should have peeled it first. He knew that monkeys could peel a banana, but could an iguana?

With a sigh he opened the door, took out the banana and started to peel it.

And that was when Iggy decided to move!

He shot out of the terrarium and across the floor. Matthew dropped the banana and tried to catch him, but Iggy was too fast. With amazing speed he shot under one of the shelves and took cover behind a plant stand. Lying on his stomach, Matthew could see the long green tail sticking out. If he reached out a hand he could grab it. . . .

He hesitated. What if Iggy didn't like being grabbed? What if he turned around and snapped at Matthew's hand? It might be better to try to coax him out with the peeled banana. Oh, if *only* he wasn't on his own! Still, at least he'd remembered to close the living-room door, so there was no risk of Iggy disappearing up the chimney.

After ten minutes of coaxing and pleading, Iggy showed no signs of coming out from his hiding place. Matthew was close to despair. How many hours would he have to lie here in this cramped position? His stomach rumbled. He was getting hungry. He looked at his watch and saw it was nearly time for supper.

Another ten minutes passed.

Still Iggy didn't move.

Another ten minutes.

Still Iggy didn't move.

The doorbell rang.

Matthew groaned with relief. "Stay there," he commanded, although it seemed unlikely that Iggy would ever move again.

He raced to the front door.

"Sorry," said Sam, breathless. "I forgot and went down to the shops. Are you okay?"

"No, I'm not!" said Matthew irritably. "Iggy got out while I was peeling a banana. And now he's hiding and I can't get hold of him. Come and see."

He led Sam through to the green-house.

"He's under that shelf," he told her.

"You'll have to get down on your stomach to see him."

Sam lay down. "I can't see anything," she said.

"Only his tail's sticking out. The rest of him is behind the plant stand."

"I can't see any tail. I don't think he's here."

"He must be. . . ." Matthew lay down and peered under the shelf.

IGGY HAD VANISHED!

"Well, he must be here somewhere." Matthew stood up. He looked around the conservatory.

"Maybe he went back in his tank," Sam suggested. "After all, that's his home."

But Iggy had not gone back into the terrarium. There was no sign of him anywhere.

"Matthew, I've just noticed something," said Sam. "The door into the living room is open. Officer Wilkins said we had to keep it closed."

"I did!" protested Matthew. "I closed it every time I . . ." His voice tailed off. Had he closed it when he went to let Sam into the house? He couldn't remember. But one thing was certain — IT WAS OPEN NOW!

They stared at each other.

Sam said slowly, "Officer Wilkins said that if he runs into the house it could take days to catch him. . . ."

Matthew gulped. "Especially if he's gone up the chimney."

They both stared at the hearth in the living room. Because it was summer there was no fire, just an arrangement of dried flowers. And it was a big, old-fashioned fireplace, plenty wide enough for an iguana on the run. . . .

"I'd better take a look," said Matthew. He moved the dried flowers out of the way and peered up the chimney.

"Can you see anything?" asked Sam.

"No, it's too dark. . . ." His voice echoed strangely in his ears. "But I think there must be something up there. Otherwise I'd be able to see the sky."

"Try this." Sam handed him a poker.

Very, very gently Matthew pushed it up the chimney. The last thing he wanted to do was startle Iggy into climbing even higher. "I can't — quite — reach," he said. "If this chimney was bigger, I could climb up it, like they did in the old days. But there isn't room. . . ."

He heard a faint noise above him.

A moment later, a small shower of soot fell on his head. Hastily he backed out of the hearth.

"Was that him?" Sam whispered fearfully.

"Must have been." Matthew wiped his forehead and stared down at the black mark on his fingers. "That's where he's gone all right, just like Officer Wilkins said."

"Oh, Matthew," said Sam. "What are we going to do?"

"Get help," said Matthew. "You go. I'll stay here. Get Jovan. Katie. My dad. Everyone. We gotta rescue Iggy from that chimney."

Chapter 6

Emergency!

By now Jovan had learned that the hamster slept most of the day but woke up in the late afternoon, when it was time for his feed. Already Hammy seemed to know him. Know him and trust him. He was perfectly happy running up Jovan's arm and perching on his shoulder.

That's where he was when the doorbell rang. Jovan stiffened. He had not left the house since yesterday for fear the bloodhound was still outside, waiting for him.

"Jo!" his mother called. "It's Sam. She says it's an emergency."

Jovan went to the door with Hammy still on his shoulder. "What's the matter?" he asked.

Sam said breathlessly, "Iggy's gone up the chimney. You've got to come."

"Sorry, I can't." He stroked Hammy's soft fur.

"You must! Matthew needs help. I've already been to his house to get Katie and his dad. *Please* come, Jo!"

Sam looked so upset that Jovan felt torn. He glanced cautiously up the path. No sign of the bloodhound.

"Oh, all right," he said. "I'll just put Hammy back in his cage, then I'll come."

They raced down the road together. As they turned the corner, they bumped into a red-haired girl. She seemed about to speak, but Sam said quickly, "Can't stop, Lucy. We've got an emergency."

As they ran past her, Jovan realized that the red-haired girl had a dog on a leash. A brown-and-white spaniel with a pointed nose . . .

"Hey, Sam," he panted. "Do you know — that girl?"

"Her name's Lucy — Tripp," panted Sam. "She — lives above the — bookstore."

Dad had said that Mrs. Tripp had a brown-and-white cocker spaniel. And the bookstore was only two streets away. The dog could have got out and followed him home because he was lost. That would explain . . .

Sam stopped dead. "Look!" she exclaimed.

Jovan looked — and what he saw drove all thoughts of spaniels and red-haired girls right out of his head.

Parked outside Officer Wilkins's house

were four vehicles:

A police car.

A fire engine.

An animal control van.

A chimney sweep's van.

He whistled under his breath. "Phew, that's the biggest emergency I've ever seen!"

Sam said unhappily, "Poor Matthew. We shouldn't have left him to petsit Iggy on his own."

Matthew's dad came to the door. "I called the fire department because they're good at rescuing cats from trees," he told them. "But of course an iguana is a bit different from a cat, so we asked animal control to help as well."

"Is Iggy still up the chimney?" asked Sam.

"I'm afraid so. We think he's probably scared and is climbing farther and farther up. That's why we sent for the chimney sweep." He opened the door to the living room. "You'd better come in."

The living room seemed full of people. Besides Matthew and Katie, there were three firemen, an animal control officer, and a chimney sweep. When Sam and Jovan entered they all turned around and said, "Sssssh!"

"We've got to keep quiet," whispered Matthew, who had a large smudge of soot on his forehead. "We don't want to frighten him."

The chimney sweep finished assembling his long brush. "Okay," he said. "I'm ready."

"Go very gently," said the animal control officer. "Having that brush come up the chimney behind him could give him a nasty shock."

"We'll go outside," said the firemen. "One of us had better climb up on the roof and wait for him to come out of the chimney."

"I'll come with you," said the animal control officer.

They left, closing the living room door behind them. Matthew's dad said grimly, "I hope this works. Frankly I don't look forward to breaking the bad news to Bill Wilkins."

Matthew looked miserable. "It's my fault. I shouldn't have left the door open."

"It's *all* our faults," said Sam. "If we'd all been here, this wouldn't have happened."

The sweep knelt down in front of the hearth. Very, very gently he began to push the brush up the chimney.

"Can you feel anything?" asked Matthew.

"Not yet," said the sweep. He dodged back quickly to avoid another fall of soot. "But this chimney badly needs sweeping. I'd better come again sometime with my full equipment."

They held their breaths as more and more of the brush disappeared up the chimney.

"Poor Iggy," said Sam. "He must be scared, up there by himself in the dark."

Matthew looked more miserable than ever.

Suddenly there was a shout from the firemen outside. Matthew's dad went to see what was happening.

Seconds later he returned.

"Is it Iggy?" asked Matthew. "Can they see him?"

"They can see the brush," said his dad. "But there's no sign of Iggy."

Chapter 7

Yummy, Yummy!

Everyone ran out into the street to look. Two firemen were holding the ladder against the side of the house, while the third fireman was on top of the roof with the animal control officer.

By now a small crowd had gathered to watch.

"What's going on?" asked a man in his shirtsleeves.

"It's that iguana that belongs to Bill Wilkins," said a woman with folded arms. "I knew there'd be trouble one day. I don't believe in keeping wild animals, myself."

Jovan felt something press against his leg and looked down to see a brown-and-white dog sniffing at his jeans. He leaped back in alarm.

"Sorry," said his owner, pulling at the leash.

Jovan recognized her at once. It was Lucy Tripp, the red-haired girl from the bookstore. "Your dog's been following me," he said accusingly. "Yesterday he followed me all the way home."

"Yes, I know." She turned rather pink. "Actually it wasn't him that followed you. It was me."

Jovan stared at her. "I thought I heard footsteps. But I didn't see *you*, only the dog."

"That's because I kept out of sight. Every time you looked round I dodged behind a hedge or a streetlight."

"Why?" asked Jovan, puzzled.

"I wanted to make sure Marcus was all right." Lucy turned even pinker. "Marcus is my hamster. I knew you'd got him because I saw you walk past our shop with him yesterday. I recognized the cage."

So that was one mystery solved — almost.

"But why did you leave him at my father's veterinary office?" Jovan asked.

"I thought he'd be safe there. I couldn't keep him at home because of Frankenstein, you see."

"Your dog?" Jovan glanced suspiciously at the spaniel.

"No, our cat," said Lucy. "Frankenstein used to crouch beside Marcus's cage, licking his lips. Poor Marcus, I knew he'd never feel safe as long as Frankenstein was around, but my mom loves Frankie and so do I, really. The only thing I could do was find another home for Marcus."

"So you don't want him back?" Jovan felt relieved, although he wasn't sure why.

"I'd love to have him back, but —"

"Jo, are you coming?" called Sam. "We're going back indoors."

"Sorry, I can't talk now," he told Lucy. "Come over to my house later, and we'll decide what to do about Hammy. I mean Marcus."

He followed the others indoors.

Everyone sat in the living room, wondering gloomily what to do next.

"The question is," said the animal control officer to Matthew, "did you actually *see* Iggy go up the chimney?"

"Well, no," said Matthew. "Not actually *see* him. No, I didn't."

"Then why were you so sure that's where he went?"

"Because it's where he went before," said Matthew. "And when I looked up the chimney I couldn't see the sky . . . and then I heard a noise and soot fell on my face."

"I'm not surprised," said the chimney sweep. "Like I said, it badly needs sweeping."

"So if Iggy didn't go up the chimney after all," said Matthew's dad, "he could be anywhere in this room. Anywhere in this *house,* for that matter."

The animal control officer stood up. "Okay," he said briskly. "We'd better start searching. You kids stay here."

Matthew started to protest. "Oh, but—"

"No arguing," said his dad. "Stay in the greenhouse and keep the door closed. We'll let you know when it's safe to come out."

Downhearted, the Petsitters went into the greenhouse and closed the door.

"What if they don't find him?" said Matthew. "Do you think we should call Officer Wilkins and ask him to come home?"

"He'll be really, really angry," said Katie in a small voice.

"This is the worst mess we've ever been in," said Sam miserably. "Oh, Matthew, I'm sorry we didn't come with you. We should never have let you do this job on your own."

"I'm sorry, too," said Jovan. "I shouldn't have let myself be scared by a cocker spaniel."

"And I shouldn't have been so stupid over the crickets," said Katie.

"That's okay," said Matthew gruffly. "I just hope they find Iggy all right."

Suddenly Jovan noticed something odd. The umbrella plant was shaking. He could see the leaves trembling as if blown by the wind. But there was no wind in the greenhouse. . . .

He looked up at the plant. Did he imagine it, or was there a strange shape clinging to the trunk? A strange, prehistoric, scaly green shape?

He cleared his throat. "Er, I think I know where he is."

Matthew stared at him. "Where?"

"Just above your head."

Everyone stared up at the plant. "He's there all right," whispered Sam. "He must have been in the greenhouse all this time. . . ."

Katie turned to the door. "I'll tell Dad. . . ."

"No, wait!" Matthew picked up the banana he had peeled earlier. "Let's try to coax him back into his tank."

He held the banana in front of Iggy. The others held their breaths.

"Come on, Iggy. Good boy. Lovely banana, yummy yummy . . ."

Slowly Iggy began to move. Inch by inch he crawled down the trunk of the umbrella plant toward the floor, following the banana Matthew was holding in front of his nose. When he reached the floor, he began to move faster — so fast that he managed to snatch a mouthful of banana. Hastily Matthew threw the rest into the terrarium, and Iggy scuttled after it. Matthew slid the door shut.

Phew! The Petsitters breathed again.

Sam opened the door into the living room. "You can stop searching," she called out. "We've found him!"

"So it turned out fine in the end," Jovan told his father when he came home that evening. "But it's taught us a lesson. Some petsitting jobs need all four of us. We can't leave it all to one person."

"Very wise," agreed Mr. Roy.

"Oh, and I found out who left Hammy — I mean Marcus — at your office. It was Lucy Tripp from the bookstore. She came over earlier to see him." Jovan stroked the hamster sitting on his shoulder.

"Does she want him back?" asked Mr. Roy.

"No, because he's scared of Frankenstein. That's her cat. But she wanted to make sure Marcus was all right, and that's why she kept following me."

"I thought it was a dog that followed you," said his mother, puzzled.

"Yes, it was. But Lucy was there too, only I never saw her because she kept out of sight." Jovan tickled Hammy under the chin. "So I'm going to look after him for her. I've said she can come and visit him whenever she likes."

"Sounds like a good idea," said Mr Roy.

Jovan nodded. Actually he thought it was a brilliant idea and so did Lucy when he suggested it. It was just another petsitting job, really. Hammy – Marcus – nibbled his ear and he grinned.

An extra-extra-long petsitting job!

The End

Join the Petsitters Club for *more* animal adventure!

Look out for:

Petsitters Summer Special: Monkey Puzzle